The XK Files: 120

Jennifer Barker

Illustrated by

Robin Lawrie

First published in the UK in 2018 by Porter Press International Ltd.
Hilltop Farm, Knighton-on-Teme, Tenbury Wells, Worcestershire,
WR15 8LY, UK

The moral rights of the author have been asserted.

A CIP catalogue record for this book will be available from
the British Library.

Printed and bound in the UK by Gomer Press.

ISBN: 978-1-907085-72-7

Cover design by Jennifer Barker

www.porterpress.co.uk

For Alex and Zoë...

...with whom every day is

an adventure!

Thank Yous:

I would like to thank my wonderful colleagues at *Porter Press International* and *The International XK Club,* particularly Philip and Julie Porter, for giving me the support, encouragement and inspiration to write this book.

Thank you to my parents, Andrew and Linda for their insights into life in the early '50s (although they were very young, of course!) and for their inspiring relationship with their grandchildren.

Finally, thank you to Robin Lawrie for his fantastic illustrations. He has brought an added visual dimension to the story with his atmospheric and evocative images.

Our story takes place in the summer of 2018, the 70th anniversary year of the launch of the Jaguar XK 120 at the London Motor Show in 1948.

This book is published as part of the XK Club's XK70 Jaguar Festival celebrations to mark the 1948 launch of this sensational, British, open-top sports car. The XK 120's large export numbers played a vital part in the revival of the British economy, following the austerity of the early post-war years.

The story is a time-travelling adventure that takes place in the historical context of these post-war years, culminating in the celebrations for Queen Elizabeth II's Coronation in 1953.

It was inspired by the author joining the Porter Press and XK Club team in July 2017 and immersing herself in the world of classic car ownership and its associated stories and history.

Chapter One
The Great Discovery

Bill had just arrived with his mum, dad, little sister Alice, grandma and grandpa at a cottage in Cornwall for his summer holiday.

"Let's build sandcastles!" Alice called excitedly. Alice set the bucket down and Bill dug in the wet – but not too wet – sand to fill it up for her.

"Tap, tap, tap!" sang Alice as they pushed the sand down. "Ta da!" Alice gasped in happiness at the perfect little castle standing on the sand before her.

"Now we have to decorate it with treasure! Let's go, Alice!" called Bill, running to the shoreline to look for some shells.

After a magical day at the beach, Bill and Alice returned sandy, exhausted, but happy, to the cottage. They were looking forward to tea, and the scones Mum had promised for pudding!

The tea was lovely. Delicious crab sandwiches, washed down with lemonade and the scones were heaped with sticky, runny jam and piled with peaks of cream.

"Can we play in the garden now?" asked Bill.

"Yes of course, although you don't have many toys here," replied Mum. "But the people who own this cottage have children. Perhaps there are some toys you can borrow in the garage. I'll find the keys."

Mum gave Bill the keys. He turned the key in the lock and crept tentatively into the old garage. It was a bit dark and dusty in there.

"There are some tennis racquets and a ball, a football and skittles!" Bill called out to his mum. He was about to step back, out of the door, when he noticed a big, shadowy shape at the back of the garage. He walked slowly towards it, wondering as he did so whether it was such a good idea. He soon realised that it was something really very large, covered with an old, dusty blanket. Carefully, he lifted up the blanket and peeped under.

Two eyes blinked in surprise at the light, opened and looked up at him, sleepily. Bill jumped back in surprise. "Hello, you've woken me up," said a voice.

"Gosh, how long have you been asleep under there?" asked Bill.

"I'm not sure, but I remember my owner tucking me up nice and cosy, under this blanket, after we'd been for a drive and I must've drifted off to sleep," replied the voice.

Slowly, Bill realised he was talking to a car!

"You're a CAR!"

"Yes, I'm a Jaguar XK 120 and I'm very thirsty. You wouldn't happen to have some petrol would you?" asked the sleepy car.

"It's nice to meet you. I think I'll just call you 'XK' for short. I'm Bill. My mum will be wondering where I am. I'd better go back now, with these toys, but I'll ask Grandpa about the petrol. He knows a lot about cars. I'll be back soon. Don't go anywhere!"

"I don't think I can," replied XK, sadly. "My engine doesn't feel quite right."

"Don't worry, XK, I'll help you," replied Bill. "My grandpa will know just what to do." Bill pulled the blanket back over XK. "You rest now, and I'll come back tomorrow with my grandpa." XK dozed back off, under his cosy blanket.

When he came out of the garage, Alice was jumping up and down, wanting to play. Bill thought he'd better play with her to keep her happy before bedtime. This was just the sort of time in the day that the slightest upset caused Alice to have what he called 'a total meltdown'.

They started to kick the ball around the garden but Bill kept missing the ball. He couldn't think about football. All he could think about was his new friend, XK, under the blanket in the garage. He couldn't wait for the opportunity to tell his grandpa all about him.

Chapter Two
Telling Grandpa

Once Alice was settled, and in her bed, it was time for Bill's story time with Mum. Grandpa had been doing story time as well some nights in the holiday. Bill really hoped that tonight would be a 'Grandpa story night' for two reasons. Firstly, he loved Grandpa's stories, which he made up especially for Bill. They usually involved cars. Secondly, he wanted some time alone with Grandpa to tell him all about XK and his wonderful discovery in the garage.

Bill was keen to get to bed, for once, to the surprise of his mum.

"Bill, you're ready already!" she exclaimed as she came into his room and saw him tucked up in his bed.

"Yes, I'm looking forward to story time tonight," replied Bill.

Mum smiled and started reading the book. Bill *did* enjoy the story; it was an exciting one about a boy having adventures on his holidays, so it was perfect holiday reading. As Mum was leaving, she said the words Bill had been hoping to hear.

"I think Grandpa wants to tell you a story tonight too." Bill beamed enthusiastically.

"Dad!" his mother called, "Bill is ready for your story now!"

Grandpa arrived in his room.

Bill loved his grandpa — he was such fun. When he went to Grandpa's house they would build and race model cars. Working together in Grandpa's workshop, they would carefully paint and assemble all the parts. Bill loved sitting side-by-side, concentrating under the light of Grandpa's old lamp he had set up for the job. Then they would head out onto the perfectly-flat patio and race them round and round for hours.

It was just like a real race and very competitive.
You had to complete a certain number of laps and
Grandpa even had a chequered flag and a podium
for the winner. Bill had lemonade, rather than
champagne though, if he was the winner.

"Hello, Bill. Are you ready for your story now?" asked Grandpa.

"Yes, I am and then I have something to tell you too, Grandpa!" replied Bill.

"Oh, I shall look forward to that, young man," replied Grandpa. He then launched into a very exciting story about a race car and its victory in an important, thrilling race for a shiny trophy.

Bill loved to watch Grandpa's face as he told the stories, as much as the stories themselves.

As he told of a daring overtaking manoeuvre and the race to the chequered flag, Grandpa became so animated. It was as though he was behind the wheel himself. "So right at the last moment, on the last straight, the car was suddenly in the lead and thundered over the line – the trophy was his!" Grandpa finished.

After the story, Grandpa said to Bill, "So what was it that you wanted to tell me?"

"I found an old car under a blanket in the garage here, Grandpa. His name is XK and he can talk," replied Bill.

"Well I never," chuckled Grandpa. "A talking car! And an XK you say? You'll have to show me that tomorrow then, Bill."

Bill knew his grandpa didn't believe what he'd told him was true. But tomorrow he would show XK to his grandpa — and he would see that it was!

Chapter Three
Adventures with XK

The next morning Bill couldn't wait to get his grandpa out to the garage to find XK. Mum had made delicious porridge with blueberries for breakfast and he wolfed it down as fast as he could. He drank his milk at an awesome speed and even refused toast when it was offered.

Grandpa, unfortunately for Bill, liked a leisurely breakfast — especially whilst on holiday. So, even though Bill was finished, he had to endure his grandpa having some of absolutely everything on offer.

He had porridge with honey, bacon, sausages, eggs, tomato, mushrooms and toast!

All washed down with not one, but two, cups of coffee and a large glass of orange juice!

When Grandpa had finally finished this utterly epic breakfast, he then wanted to go and brush his teeth!

"But Grandpa, remember, I've got something to show you!"

"Yes, yes, Bill I haven't forgotten. But, you've got to look after your teeth, especially at my age!" He merrily went off to the bathroom, humming happily as he went. Bill tried to be patient, but it seemed to him that Grandpa was in there for ages - an eternity - longer even than double history, his least favourite subject! Finally, Grandpa emerged from the bathroom, beaming with a big grin to show off his newly-polished teeth.

"So then, Bill, let's go to the garage."

Grandpa went back downstairs and took the garage keys off the little hook in the kitchen. They crossed over the grassy lawn. With the dew twinkling in the summer morning sunshine it was like a jewelled carpet, leading to treasure inside.

When they arrived at the garage, Grandpa put the key in the lock and Bill's heart thumped with anticipation and excitement at seeing XK again. They went into the shadowy garage and Bill began to walk towards the largest shadow of all – the one he knew to be XK.

"Hang on a moment, Bill, I think there's a light switch here," called out his grandpa. And sure enough, as Grandpa flicked the switch, the garage was suddenly illuminated from an enormous strip light on the ceiling. It was easy to see the way to the back of the garage now.

"Over here, Grandpa," said Bill, leading the way. They approached the blanketed car.

Bill slowly and gently lifted the blanket, as he had done the previous day. And, just as before, two eyes blinked up at them – even more startled this time by the glare from the strip light.

"Bill, it's you!" said XK, a bit shocked and sleepy but nonetheless pleased to see him again.

"Yes, and here's my grandpa." Bill turned to look at his Grandpa. His jaw was wide open and he looked totally astonished, as though he couldn't quite believe what he could see.

Full of uncertainty at speaking to a car, Grandpa asked hesitantly, "Are... are.. are... are... you a Jaguar XK 120?"

"Yes, I am," replied XK, proudly.

"But I like to call him XK for short," said Bill.

Grandpa looked through the dusty, grimy windscreen and into the car, as though looking for clues to explain this curious phenomenon. He saw leather seats, tattered and torn but which looked fine to sit on.

"Do you mind if we get in, to have a look

inside?" asked Grandpa. "I've always wanted to sit in a Jaguar XK 120."

"Of course you can, go ahead," replied XK.

Grandpa carefully opened the door. It was rather stiff, from not being opened for many years. He then opened the passenger door and let Bill in, closing the door very gently after him. Then he walked back round to the driver's door and let himself in, again with great care.

When Grandpa closed the door, with a gentle **clunk**, something strange and amazing happened. Suddenly the leather seats, in which they were sitting, looked shiny and new again — polished, gleaming, spick-and-span, as though they had been recently fitted in XK.

The instrument dials were no longer tarnished but bright and shiny. The interior of the car looked brand new! Also, rather thrillingly for Bill, and somewhat worryingly for Grandpa, as he was in the driver's seat, there was noise from the engine. They seemed to be moving. They were travelling along a road, in what must have been a town or city because they could make out the large shapes of buildings and lots of street lamps. But it was hard to see, there was a cloudy swirl of what seemed like heavy fog surrounding them as they drove. Suddenly, there was a gap in the clouds and they could see properly.

They were in London.

Chapter Four
London

"XK," said Bill, "can you still hear us?"

"Oh yes," replied the voice.

"And are *you* driving?" Grandpa quickly asked.

"Yes, I am," said XK.

"Oh, good," replied Grandpa, "because I'm not and I was wondering who was!"

Bill looked around him in wonder. There were quite a few other, old-fashioned cars on the road, but not many and certainly not very many for a street in London.

He had been there to visit his aunt and knew what the hustle and bustle of a London street normally looked like.

As they moved along the street, Bill could see that lots of the buildings had crumbled. There were teams of builders at every turn working to repair and rebuild them. Lots of men in uniform were walking around the streets. It was an unusual sight for Bill to see so many soldiers and he wondered why they were all there.

They passed a horse, pulling a red Royal Mail

cart behind him. At the next turn, there was a
more familiar-looking red double-decker London
bus. It looked old-fashioned to Bill, but not as
strange as the horse and cart on the road.

As they passed the entrance to a park, Grandpa suddenly gasped.

"Why, that's mother and I!" Grandpa pointed at a little boy, marching down the street in his shorts, braces and long socks, holding tightly to his mum's hand.

At the gates to the park, they were met by a tall man in a suit and tie, wearing a bowler hat. The man smiled when he saw the woman and child, took the boy's outstretched hand and walked into the park. "And that's my father — your great grandfather, Bill. We used to live near here," remembered Grandpa, in total astonishment at what he was seeing. "I look about three. I think XK has brought us back to London in 1949!"

XK pulled over, close to the wrought iron
fences enclosing the park, and Bill and Grandpa
were able to watch as the family played in the
park. Grandpa's father was kicking a football to
and fro with him.

"My father, your great grandfather, worked in a bank after the second world war. Before that, he was a pilot in the war and helped to fight the Luftwaffe, the German air force, in the skies above London, France and Germany. I was born a year after the war ended. London had been hit by lots of bombs during the war and, as you can see around you, the rebuilding of London took many years to complete. It's four years after the war ended and there are still lots of unrepaired places," explained Grandpa.

Grandpa's mother, Bill's great grandmother, then began unpacking a picnic.

"Ah, we have bread, but I bet there's not any meat in those sandwiches," said Grandpa, watching from the car.

"Why not, Grandpa?" asked Bill. "Well, meat was still rationed and very hard to get hold of. We had it sometimes, but mainly just for Sunday lunch," explained Grandpa.

"Rationing was put in place in the war, as food was scarce and had to be shared around equally to be fair so everyone could survive. People turned their gardens into allotments and were told to 'Dig for Victory'. Growing your own food was seen as a good thing to do to help the war effort. Public parks like this one were turned into big allotments too. You can see some vegetable plots over there," said Grandpa, pointing to them.

"Rationing of some things continued after the war," so that's why they are still there and being used." Bill saw Grandpa's mother give him a sweet.

"But sweets had come off rationing that year," said Grandpa with a smile.

"Sweets were rationed?!" questioned Bill in horror at the very thought of it.

"Oh, yes. You couldn't just walk into a shop and buy anything you wanted back then, you know," laughed Grandpa. "But then, after just a few months in that year, sweets went back on to rationing again as people were eating too many! They were worried that the sugar would run out!"

"Petrol was still rationed too," said XK, "and I didn't have much left in my tank on this day in 1949. I think we'd better go back now. If I run out, you may get stranded in 1949."

Grandpa and Bill took one last long look at the family, happily eating their lunch in the park. "We'll come back and I'll show you some more tomorrow," promised XK, as he started the engine.

They set off again down the road. Suddenly,

the fog swirled around them once more. Bill felt the wheels stop turning and heard the engine get quieter and quieter, as though a car was going off into the distance. Then, just as suddenly as they had left, they were back in the garage and the present day.

"Bill! Are you coming down to the beach?" called his mother from the door to the house.

"Yes please!" replied Bill, realising with happiness that it was exactly the same time as when they had left this morning.

That meant he'd have a full day of fun at the beach too! He grabbed his swimming trunks, towel and bodyboard and raced after Alice and his mum.

"I think I'll stay here and have a closer look round XK," Grandpa told Bill. "Tell your mum I'll join you at the beach later."

Chapter Five
Grandpa's Old House

Bill was just as eager to get to the garage the following day — and this time so was Grandpa!

They finished breakfast in double-quick time and crossed the lawn to the garage as fast as they could. Lifting the blanket, they woke XK who opened his eyes and smiled up at them.

"Oh, hello! Are you ready for another drive?"

"Yes please!" replied Bill, eagerly. They climbed into the seats and again the fog was surrounding them. It seemed even thicker this time.

"It's a right peasouper this one," said his grandpa.

"What's a peasouper, Grandpa?" asked Bill, looking around, half expecting to see green liquid bubbling on a hob somewhere.

"A peasouper is a really thick fog mixed with smoke from coal fires and factories," explained Grandpa. "We had lots of them in London when I was a child. Most things were powered by coal back then. It caused a lot of pollution in the air."

The fog didn't seem to be clearing as quickly as it had on their first journey. "XK, I think we need headlights," said Grandpa quickly. XK put on his lights and it was a little better, but they still couldn't see much. "This must be one of the really bad ones," said Grandpa.

They suddenly saw that they were outside a house. "That's the house I used to live in with my parents!" exclaimed Grandpa in astonishment. XK pulled up by the kerb.

"Yes, I told you I'd show you more," replied XK.

From the street, they could see into the front room. They could just make out Grandpa's mother coming in and out of the room.

"I wonder if she can see us?" said Bill. He was keen to get out of the car and take a closer look.

"I don't think they will be able to see you," said XK. "I get the feeling that the people in the other cars can't see me on the road! Why don't you go closer and find out?" Bill didn't need asking twice! He opened his car door and stepped out onto the pavement.

Walking up to the window, he felt a little unsure, like he was doing something he shouldn't but his curiosity got the better of him. It's not like I'm spying or anything. I'm sure if they knew about me, I would be most welcome to look. After all, I am family!

As he approached the window, it was clear that his great grandmother couldn't see him. She looked straight towards the window and her face didn't register anything. It was like she was looking through him. It was like being a ghost, walking around unseen, thought Bill. But a ghost from the future rather than the past. It was a very strange feeling indeed.

Bill looked around the front room. He could see his grandpa, older now — about six, playing on the floor with his toys. Bill also noticed that there was a television in the room. It looked like a small wooden box with a screen made of curved, thick glass. Bill only recognised it as a television because of the moving pictures on the screen.

Bill heard music and an old black and white children's TV show started. The name of the show then came on screen, *Muffin the Mule*.

"Ah, this was my favourite," said Grandpa, appearing at his side. "I look about six. This show is on television and I think this must be the Great Smog of London. It's 1952," he said thoughtfully, looking around at the thick, thick smog that still surrounded them.

The young Grandpa suddenly looked up at the window and waved. "He can see us!" exclaimed Bill. Grandpa noticed that his younger self was looking straight at him — it was a very odd feeling. He didn't look upset or frightened by the faces at the window; it was as though he knew them. The people he saw were very familiar to him somehow and comforting. The little boy looked very happy and carried on playing as though there was nothing strange about it.

Suddenly, a slightly older girl entered the room, she looked about eight. "It's Charlotte! My sister, Charlotte, and I had both been kept inside and couldn't play out. That's why we're watching this and playing with toys in the front room. Mother kept us in the house because the smog was so bad."

When Charlotte saw what was on the television, she went straight over to sit by Bill, without taking her eyes off the screen. She didn't look up at the window.

Bill realised that the smog wasn't bothering him at all. He hadn't coughed once — another effect from being a ghost from the future he supposed. It was as though he was there, but not fully there.

He looked around at the other people walking down the street. Some had masks on to protect them from the smog. Strips of white material were over their mouths and noses, held in place with loops of elastic over their ears. Not one passer-by even glanced at XK. Bill then knew that XK was right - *they* couldn't see XK either. A splendid car like XK would certainly have had people looking at him — smog or no smog!

"I think it might be time we went," called XK from by the kerb. "The smog is getting even thicker now that it's getting towards evening. Although I have plenty of fuel, as the petrol rationing has ended, I need to make sure I can see well enough to drive," explained XK. Bill and Grandpa nodded.

"The TV will be turned off soon anyway, when it gets to teatime, Bill," said Grandpa, seeing that Bill was enjoying the show. "There was only one channel back then and children's programmes were only on for an hour, once a day."

"One channel? An hour? Is that all?!" exclaimed Bill, thinking of all the channels and TV shows he could watch — not to mention DVDs, computer games and the tablet he had as emergency back-up if he couldn't find anything good on TV.

"Things certainly were different for you growing up, Grandpa," said Bill, thoughtfully, as he followed Grandpa back to XK. They got in and again the fog swirled round and round as they started to drive. Then suddenly it cleared, once more, and they were back in the garage.

Chapter Six
Coronation

The next morning, Grandpa told Bill that he had contacted the owners of the cottage and told them about finding XK. At first Bill was worried.

"Will that mean our adventures will stop, Grandpa?" Bill asked.

"Well, Bill, we are only here for another week and a half anyway. I think it was only right to tell them that we've had a look around their car. I told them that we sat inside it too, and they didn't mind. I left out the bit about it talking *and* going back in time — I think you really have to see that for yourself to believe it."

Bill nodded in relief.

He was pleased that he and Grandpa were the only ones who knew about *that*.

"I sat in XK by myself and nothing happened. *You* seem to be the key, Bill. The key XK needs to drive us into the past," explained Grandpa.

Bill was really pleased.

Being the key to a magical, time-travelling car was just the sort of adventure Bill had dreamed of having this summer! It was so exciting to think that he was the only one that could make XK drive back into the past. It made Bill feel very proud.

"I know a man who restores old cars, particularly cars like this one," continued Grandpa. "XK's owners asked me to contact him on their behalf to look into repairing XK. It would be lovely to see him out of the garage and back on the road, wouldn't it?"

Bill nodded in agreement again.

"But for now, let's see where he's going to take us today shall we?" said Grandpa.

"Don't you mean *when*?" replied Bill.

"I suppose I do!" agreed Grandpa.

When the fog cleared *this* time, Bill found it was much easier to see. They were driving on a street in London again and it was brighter and clearer, but raining. As Bill looked around him, he could see red, white and blue bunting and union jack flags hanging from lots of buildings. Golden cardboard cut-out crowns flapped in the breeze.

Some of the smaller side streets had long tables, covered with tablecloths and with rows of chairs on each side, set up in the middle of the road! It was as though the most ginormous dinner, ever, was about to take place in the middle of the street! Everything looked very jolly.

"We must be in 1953 — it's Coronation Day," said Grandpa, joyfully.

Just then, Bill caught sight of young Grandpa. He was dressed in smart trousers, shirt and a jumper. His sister was standing next to him in a smart skirt, shirt and jumper with her hair tied back with a red and white ribbon in a big bow. "We're in our best clothes for the party," said Grandpa.

Lots of people suddenly started arriving at Grandpa's house, all dressed up as well. "Why are so many people going in to your house?" asked Bill, surprised at this procession of visitors.

"Well, we were one of the only houses in the neighbourhood to have a TV," said Grandpa.

"Really?!" replied Bill.

"Yes, TVs were still a very new thing. People still mostly listened to the radio in those days. Everyone has come to see the new queen, Queen Elizabeth II, be crowned at Westminster Abbey. It is going to be on television, so they've come to watch it with us. It's the first time *ever* a king or queen has had a coronation on television."

Bill suddenly noticed that young Grandpa had

something in his hand. It looked like a coin in a little box.

"What's that you're holding?" asked Bill.

"Ah, that's my Coronation coin. I was given it as a souvenir of the day. I think I still have it somewhere. I'll show you when you're next over at my house."

Young Grandpa and Charlotte followed the visitors into the room. Bill looked through the window. He couldn't believe how many people were in the front room! "I think we could go in too. I don't think anyone can see us, except me when I was younger, and there are so many people. I think it would be OK to stand at the back and watch," said Grandpa.

The TV coverage was about to start.

Everyone watched as The Queen travelled down The Mall, past Trafalgar Square and along the Thames Embankment in an ornate golden horse-drawn coach to Westminster Abbey. She was surrounded by dozens of footmen and guards on horseback. Big crowds of people lined the streets and schoolchildren, gathered on a corner, cheered loudly and waved their handkerchiefs as

The Queen passed by. Men waved their bowler hats in the air.

The picture looked very shaky and grainy to Bill and he couldn't see much on the tiny screen everyone was huddled around, even though a magnifying glass had been placed in front of it. But he realised the importance of the occasion and so watched intently.

He did notice that young Grandpa, being only six, was easily distracted by his *Beano* comic.

At times during the service, he preferred to read the adventures of *Dennis the Menace* than watch. After all, the service was really, really long! Bill smiled at this. He loved *The Beano* too! It seemed some things were just the same for his grandpa growing up.

Everyone in the room was hushed as The Queen entered the Abbey to the sound of singing. They all watched as she slowly walked down the carpet in the centre of the church to sit on the throne. The Queen said some words promising to serve the United Kingdom and other countries of which she was to be queen. She put on a huge golden coat before sitting in a very old throne belonging to King Edward and was given a sword — then another huge robe. It must've been very heavy! Bill thought it was a good job she was sitting down on that throne. The Archbishop then put the orb, sceptre and rod into The Queen's hands, one after the other, and placed the crown on her head.

Then everyone chanted, "Long live The Queen! Long live The Queen! Long live The Queen!" both in the Abbey and in the room with the television.

Everyone in the room gave a loud cheer. The Queen was crowned.

The Queen then left the Abbey, with her ladies-in-waiting holding the train of her cloak up off the floor. She left to the sound of the National Anthem. Lots of people in young Grandpa's living room sang that too! She got back in her coach and returned to Buckingham Palace. Bill watched as members of the Royal Family, Prime Ministers and kings and queens of other countries all followed The Queen out of the Abbey. When she got back to Buckingham Palace, she appeared on a balcony above the huge crowds gathered below.

Bill could see that the crowd of people gathered outside the Palace all cheered when The Queen appeared. She waved at the crowds and there were more cheers. Then she turned and went back into the Palace.

"Now it's time for the street party," said Grandpa, happily. "Come on, let's go and see!"

Chapter Seven
Espionage

They followed everyone out into the street. The tables were piled high with food. There were plenty of treats, as sugar rationing had ended again — this time for good!

Bill saw that all the children had a special mug with The Queen's face, flags, flowers, a crown and the date of the Coronation on it. Grandpa saw him looking at them and explained, "We were all given a special mug at school to mark the occasion of the Coronation. I think I still have that somewhere too." People started to take their seats at the table.

Bill suddenly noticed three men in the street, whispering urgently to each other. There was something about their behaviour which struck Bill as unusual. Realising that they wouldn't be able to see him, he went closer to the little group to see if he could hear what they were saying.

As he got closer, he heard one of them say, "Yes, we will get you the information you need. Everyone is distracted by the Coronation today, it will be easy. It's the perfect cover for this operation." The second man then nodded.

"Good, contact me when you have it and we will arrange to meet again," said the third man.

Bill noticed that the third man spoke with a foreign accent. He thought it sounded Russian.

He rushed over to tell Grandpa what he had heard. "Sounds like they might be up to no good," said Grandpa, after hearing what had been said. "I think we should follow them. They won't be able to see us if we do. Quickly, let's get to XK!"

Bill noticed that two of the men, but not the one with the foreign accent, were getting into a car to drive away.

"Quick, Grandpa, I think they are going," he gasped, urgently. They ran and got into XK. "We need to follow that car, XK," said Bill, pointing at the car the men were in. "We cannot lose them."

"We'll follow the other man," said a voice, suddenly at the door. It was young Grandpa and Charlotte. They had heard everything!

"You can *both* see and hear us?" asked Bill in total surprise.

"Yes, Charlotte can see you too," replied young Grandpa. Charlotte nodded seriously and then smiled at them. The Rusian man was setting off on foot down the road.

"OK, follow him and see where he goes but don't go too far from home. And stay out of sight," urged Grandpa, as they quickly drove away to follow the other two men's car.

Grandpa, Bill and XK set off through the streets of London after the car. They travelled along the side of Kensington Gardens — where they had first seen young Grandpa. Then they followed the car down Exhibition Road, along the route set up around the *Coronation Area*. This was an area which was closed to all traffic for the Coronation.

Bill could see crowds and crowds of people walking around, dressed in their finest, smart clothes.

The car passed The Natural History Museum and Bill remembered going there with his aunt, to see the dinosaurs, when he had last visited her. Bill thought of the big bones of the dinosaurs inside and wondered if they had been there when Grandpa was a boy.

He knew that they were really old, of course, but didn't know if they had been dug up from the ground yet in 1953. There was no time to check!

They carried on and drove along the side of the River Thames, past Chelsea Bridge and arrived at Vauxhall Bridge. Here, the two men parked their car and got out to walk. Bill and Grandpa were able to follow them in XK, as no one could see either them or the car. It was a very strange feeling, crossing the empty bridge and driving along the car-free roads.

The men walked North, following the crowds heading towards The Mall to catch a glimpse of the new queen appearing on the balcony again. But, before they reached St James' Park and The Mall, the men took a turning. Bill could see the huge dome of Westminster Abbey and its bells were still ringing out for the Coronation.

They followed the men along Broadway, where they suddenly stopped outside a plain, brick office building with the sign *Peakpoint Fire Extinguisher Company* outside. They didn't need to keep their distance as the men could not see them, or XK, so they pulled in and parked right outside the door.

"I know this building," said XK. "I've been here lots of times before."

Meanwhile, back at the street party, young Grandpa and Charlotte had followed the Russian man to a red telephone box at the end of their road. They kept their distance and just watched, as he opened the door and went inside.

He fed lots of coins into the slot in the box above the telephone and turned the dial on the front to call the number. He waited, then pushed a button marked 'A' when the other person answered the call. He talked to the other person for a few minutes but young Grandpa and Charlotte couldn't hear what he was saying.

Charlotte could hear enough to tell that he was speaking in a foreign language. She knew they wouldn't be able to understand what he was saying even if they had been any closer.

Then the man came out of the telephone box and walked over to another car. He got in and drove away. That was that, they couldn't follow him anymore, so they started to turn to walk back up the street to the party.

"Wait a minute!" called young Grandpa. "Let's check he used all his coins."

They ran into the telephone box and Charlotte pressed the 'B' button. This was something they'd done many times before, at this phone box, to get money for sweets since the rationing of them had ended.

It was an unwritten rule, amongst the children on the street, that you *never* passed this telephone box without checking there were no unused coins to be returned!

Sure enough, the man hadn't used all the coins he had put in. A few tumbled out into Charlottes's hand. Young Grandpa was pleased. It had been well worth returning to check.

Chapter Eight
Headquarters

Back outside the building on Broadway, Bill and
Grandpa had followed the men inside. The men
had used a key; they hadn't broken in. Bill and
Grandpa slid in behind them, as the men
entered through the open door, totally
unseen.

The two men looked quickly
around, to check no-one had
seen them come in, and
walked quickly over to
a door. Bill and
Grandpa
swiftly
followed
them.

The door opened onto a stairway and the men started to climb the stairs quickly.

They knew where they were going and were moving rapidly, so Bill and Grandpa picked up their speed to keep up. They went up and up for what seemed like many, many floors. Finally, they arrived at the floor they wanted and opened the door to exit the stairway.

Bill and Grandpa followed them, sliding through the door again before it closed. They found themselves out on a long corridor, with lots of doors leading off it.

The men proceeded quickly along the corridor, looking at the numbers (there were no names) on each door as they passed them. Bill and Grandpa followed quickly after them. Bill was pleased that they wouldn't be able to hear them, as he was panting heavily after all those stairs!

Suddenly, the men stopped when they found the door they were looking for. They opened it and went inside, with Bill and Grandpa following closely behind.

Bill and Grandpa lodged themselves in the corner of the room, opposite the door. They instinctively wanted to keep out of the way, even though they couldn't be seen. Bill wasn't sure what would happen if they moved or knocked something. Would it move or fall? And would the men be able to *see* it move or fall?

They watched the two men go over to an old, large, very grand, mahogany desk sitting in the middle of this rather plain office. They pulled at the drawers, trying to open them, but they were locked shut.

"Where do you think he keeps the key?" one of the men hissed to the other.

"Not sure, let's look around the office for it." They started to search on the shelves behind the desk.

"Ah ha! Got it!" said one of them, sitting

down at the desk to upturn a little vase. The key popped out into his hand.

Bill beckoned to Grandpa that they should move behind the desk, so they could see what was going on a bit better. They shuffled along the side wall, past the window overlooking the road below. Bill looked out and down, where he could see XK waiting for them in the street below. Arriving at the back wall, they turned to see what the men were taking out of the desk drawers.

One of the men was flicking through files in a deep drawer on one side of the desk. The other said, "Quickly, find it, so we can get out of here. He might come into work today, even though it's a holiday — you never know with him."

As the man searched, Bill's eyes went to the top of the desk, looking for clues as to whose office this was. His eye came to a photograph on the desk and he couldn't help himself; he gasped. For there, on the desk, was a picture of a man in a suit and a woman in a dress and hat, standing beside a gleaming new car. That car was XK!

Grandpa heard his gasp and looked at him. Bill started pointing frantically at the photograph.

"It's XK!" he whispered. Grandpa looked at the photograph and then back at Bill, he nodded with a look of total surprise on his face.

Bill wondered whether the man in the photograph was the man who worked in this room. It seemed likely.

"Here it is!" said one of the men. He held a pale brown folder above his head and was waving it around triumphantly. On the front of the file was the title *Operation Excavation*.

"At last!" sighed the other man, snatching it from his hand. "Let's see what's inside then."

Bill and Grandpa watched the man pulling pieces of paper out of the file and laying them out on the desk. From what Bill could make out, they were letters, reports of what was said at meetings, office memos and there were some blue drawings on one. They were technical drawings, the kind used for plans to build something.

The man took a tiny camera out of his top pocket and began taking photographs of the sheets of paper, one by one. He then quickly put them back in order and placed them back in the folder.

Just as he was about to put the file back in the drawer, he noticed something else in it. He put his hand in and pulled out something that looked a bit like a roll of ribbon to Bill. But the ribbon on it was made of thin brown plastic with little square shapes on it.

"That's microfilm," Grandpa whispered to Bill.

"I think we should take this and give it to them too," said the man, slipping it into his pocket along with his camera. "Now let's get out of here," he continued.

He closed the drawer and turned the key to lock it again. Then he placed the key back in its little vase and returned it to the shelf.

Bill and Grandpa followed the men out of the room, back along the corridor, down the stairs and out of the front door. The men locked the door behind them as they left. They then walked down Broadway to a phone box at the end of the road. They got in and Bill and Grandpa pressed their ears to the glass to hear what was said.

The voice was muffled, through the glass, but they could just make out the words, "Yes we have it. We will leave it at eleven hundred hours tomorrow at the usual drop point." He placed the receiver back down and the two men left the phone box.

"I'll meet you at Knightsbridge tube station tomorrow at 10.30. I'll go back now for the car," said the man who had spoken on the phone.

"Okay, I'll see you then," said the other. He pulled his hat down over his eyes slightly and walked away. The other man, lowering his hat a little too, walked off in the other direction.

Bill and Grandpa looked at one another, shocked at what they had seen and heard.

What were these two men up to?

"Let's get back to XK, we can talk about all this with him. I have a feeling *he* might be able to tell us whose office that was," said Grandpa.

Chapter Nine
Revelations

Bill and Grandpa opened the doors and climbed into XK. "I think we should get back to my old house and find out what Charlotte and I found out about the other man," said Grandpa. "We can talk on the way."

They set off back to Kensington.

"Who do you think those men were, Grandpa?" asked Bill.

"I have a feeling they might be spies, Bill," replied his grandpa. Bill was astonished.

"Spies?" he gasped in amazement.

"Yes, and I think that building is where they usually work every day, because they had a key.

"But today they shouldn't have been there. Today is a public holiday for the Coronation. No-one went to work on this day; everyone had the day off. Today, they were here for an unusual reason. We've got to find out why." Bill nodded.

"I don't think they should've been in that office and taken what they did," continued Grandpa. "I certainly don't think they should be arranging to meet with someone and give them the information and plans from that file," said Grandpa.

"XK, you said you'd been to that building lots of times before when we first arrived," said Bill, suddenly remembering what the car had said earlier.

"We saw a photograph of a man and a woman standing next to you, in a photo frame, on a desk, in an office, in that building. Do you know anything about whose office that was?" asked Bill.

There was a pause and then XK said, "That's right! I remember now! I used to come here nearly every day with my first owner. He worked here, I think. We would come early each morning and he would park me in an underground car park. I would stay there until he returned at the end of the day. Then we would drive back to his house. I think he might have been an important person here. Sometimes we would go out in the day for meetings around London, at other buildings — hotels and restaurants too. He had a reserved car parking space in the car park and I get the feeling he was in charge," answered XK.

"We must have just been in the office of your first owner, XK! How incredible!" exclaimed Bill.

"XK, do you think you could remember the way to that man's house?" asked Grandpa.

"Yes, I think I probably could. I did the drive so often back then," replied XK.

"Good," said Grandpa. "After we've found out what the others know, we'll come back here and you can take us to his house."

They were just passing behind Buckingham Palace again and Bill thought of the new Queen inside, celebrating her Coronation at a party in the Palace with all those people who had been at the service in Westminster Abbey.

They passed Hyde Park and Kensington Gardens and arrived back in the street where Grandpa once lived. The party there was still going on. Everyone was sitting at the long table, with empty plates in front of them. The children all wore golden crown party hats on their heads and looked very happy after all that cake!

Bill saw young Grandpa and Charlotte and waved to them. They waved back.

"Who are you waving at?" asked their mother,

Bill's great grandma, who was sitting beside them.

"Oh... er... no-one... er... we're just waving because we are so happy about the new Queen," Charlotte said, quickly.

Their mother looked puzzled but seemed to accept it and turned to talk to the boy sitting next to her.

"Please may we leave the table, Mother?" asked Charlotte. "We've finished our tea and want to go and play." Their mother turned back to look at Charlotte and nodded in agreement.

They left the table to go over to where Bill and Grandpa were standing.

"Who are you?" asked Charlotte. "And why are *we* the only ones who can see you?"

Grandpa looked a little concerned. Bill could see that he was worried about telling the boy he was face-to-face with his older self. Bill decided it was better to be a little bit vague about who they really were.

"We are relatives of yours from the future. This car," he pointed at XK, "has brought us back into the past for some reason. I think that reason has something to do with those men we followed," explained Bill. "I think there's something we need to do, here in the past, something very important." Charlotte and young Grandpa nodded, trying to take in all this unusual news.

"But who *are* those men?" asked Charlotte.

"We're not sure, but we think they are spies," replied Grandpa.

"Spies?!" gasped young Grandpa, his eyes as wide as saucers. He looked very excited at this

news. "You mean Charlotte and I have followed a real-life spy!" he exclaimed.

"Well, we are not sure the man *you* followed was a spy," replied Bill, "but we think the ones *we* followed were. What did the other man do after we left?"

Charlotte and young Grandpa explained about the phone call and the fact that they were too far away to hear what was said. "We wouldn't have understood what he said anyway," said Charlotte, "he was speaking in a foreign language."

Grandpa nodded. "We think he is Russian. He must have gone to the phone box to call someone, perhaps his boss, to tell them what the other two men had offered to get for them today. I think those men are British spies who are giving secret plans for something to the Russian man," explained Grandpa.

"We must try to stop them. I think the best person to help us is XK's first owner. I think he must be the head of the Secret Intelligence Service, that's the name given to the top secret government department in charge of spies. We must find a way to show him what these two men are up to. They should be working for him but are really working for the Russian man. We know that they are meeting tomorrow to take the secrets to the Russian man. We must make sure XK's first owner is there and sees what they are doing."

Bill thought that sounded like a very good plan.

"Bill, you and I should go with XK now to see if he can find his way to his old owner's house," said Grandpa. "We will come back and tell you what we've seen," Grandpa promised Charlotte and young Grandpa. They nodded and ran back to play with their friends in the street.

The children had skipping ropes, toy cars, yo-yos, jacks, marbles and balls. They were all playing happily together out in the street, as their parents chatted and drank lots of cups of tea. Tea rationing had ended and the grown-ups were making up for it now!

Bill saw that one of the girls had a puppet on her hand. He recognised it as *Sooty* — he loved that show! He hadn't realised it was on TV when Grandpa was young!

He noticed that some of the children had made little ramps out of wooden planks and were climbing some of their toy soldiers up them and saying, "We've reached the top!" Grandpa also noticed them doing this and smiled.

"The same day that The Queen was crowned, an expedition of climbers reached the top of Everest, the world's tallest mountain, for the very first time. The children have heard the news and are playing a game about it," explained Grandpa.

Bill was enjoying watching the children play but his grandpa said, "Bill we must go now. We have to see if XK can take us to his first owner's house before it gets dark tonight."

Chapter Ten
XK's Old Garage

Bill and Grandpa returned to XK.

"Right, XK, let's go back to the office building and then you can see if you can find the way to where you lived all those many years ago," said Grandpa.

"I'll certainly try," said XK, starting his engine.

They drove through the streets of central London once more, still with no cars around but plenty of people on the pavements.

As they approached Buckingham Palace, Bill heard the roar of cheers from what sounded like a huge crowd of people in the near distance. He cupped his hand over his ear so he could hear more clearly. The crowd then started to chant, "We want The Queen! We want The Queen!" Then there was a huge roar from the crowd. Bill suddenly heard a loud rumbling in the sky. He looked up and just saw a formation of army jet planes soar through the sky.

"It's the RAF flypast!" laughed Grandpa. "The Queen and the rest of the Royal Family must be out on the balcony at Buckingham Palace to watch it."

Bill was amazed. He wished he could see The Queen, but they were at the back of the Palace, with no clear view of the royal balcony. Again, there was no time for a detour. They were heading for their important destination.

When they arrived back at the office building in Broadway, they parked by the pavement again.

"Right, here we are, XK. Can you take us to where your first owner lived in 1953?" asked Grandpa. There was a pause, as though XK was considering the question very carefully.

"Yes, I think I can," he replied. Pulling away from the kerb, he headed to Parliament Square.

Bill could see the huge tower of Big Ben and the Houses of Parliament in front of them. They turned left up Parliament Street and Bill saw the entrance to Downing Street. He wondered if the Prime Minister, Winston Churchill, whom he'd seen on the television at the Coronation earlier, was back at home with his feet up or still at the party in the Palace.

They carried on, past the towering Nelson's Column in Trafalgar Square and the solid, grey imposing National Gallery with its impressive-looking columns, perched on high overlooking the whole square. Then they turned onto Shaftesbury Avenue.

Driving past the famous theatres, they reached Piccadilly Circus with its huge advertising messages stretching across what seemed like every inch of the buildings. Bill could see logos for *Coca Cola*, *Guinness*, *Bovril*, *Schweppes* and *Wrigley's Chewing Gum* emblazoned across the walls in huge letters.

It looked very different to the huge modern screens with their moving images that Bill had seen here during his last visit to London. The new signs he had seen were mostly for technology and mobile phone companies, but Bill realised that *Coca Cola* had been there and in pretty much the same place as he could see it now. Again, it showed him that some things in the past were very different and others not so different at all.

The statue of Eros in the middle of Piccadilly Circus was encased in a pretty birdcage decoration with a crown at the top for the Coronation. They carried on down Regent Street.

Bill was pleased to see *Hamleys* toyshop — definitely one of his most favourite places in London to visit.

With its windows full of dolls, games, model cars, train sets, musical instruments and tricycles, it didn't look that different either. Bill could see children stopping to gaze in wonder at the windows full of the latest toys, just as *he* always did when he visited the shop.

They turned off Regent Street and drove past Claridges Hotel. Bill could see a doorman, standing in a suit and top hat at the grand entrance, welcoming guests through the big doors of the famous hotel. Then they turned right, then left and pulled up outside a house on Park Street.

"This is it," said XK. "We're here."

Now that they'd arrived, Bill wasn't sure what they were going to do. How could they tell XK's owner about what was going on if he couldn't see them or hear what they were saying?

It was as though Grandpa could read his thoughts because he suddenly said, "I think the best thing is to go to the garage and see if we can find XK from the past. We may be able to talk to *him* as well."

"Yes, good idea, Grandpa, let's do that," agreed Bill. They got out of XK and stood on the pavement in front of the grand, tall townhouse. There was a little garage to the side of the front door with its own small garage door.

Just then, in a stroke of good fortune, the door to the garage opened and the man from the photograph in the office was standing inside the garage. Bill could see XK was inside too.

It seemed very strange to be able to see him both inside the garage *and* outside by the pavement. But Bill didn't have much time to think about it as Grandpa whispered urgently, "Quick, Bill, let's go in!" They quickly ducked through the garage door on the opposite side to where XK's owner was standing, just as he lowered the door and locked it from the outside.

Bill was worried when he heard the lock turn.

"But, Grandpa, how are we going to get out again?" he asked.

"Don't worry, Bill," said Grandpa, pointing to a big double handle on the back of the garage door. "If we turn this from the inside, that will let us out," he reassured Bill.

"Phew! That's alright then," sighed Bill, relieved to hear that they weren't trapped after all.

They walked over to *this* XK, the one from the past who didn't know them yet. As Bill got closer to the car, the same thing happened as had in the holiday cottage garage. The car's headlamps suddenly became eyes and he looked at Bill, blinking in surprise. Then the two lines of his front bumpers joined in a large, surprised, 'o' shape.

Then he spoke.

"Oh, who are you? And what are you doing here in my garage? And... why am I talking?" said Original XK, the one from the past, with much puzzlement.

Bill thought this last question was so funny that he had to stop himself from laughing — which was very hard. But it wouldn't have done to laugh. The poor car was really confused and they had a great deal of explaining to do.

"I'm Bill and this is my grandpa," started Bill in explanation. "We have come here from the future. I found you sixty-five years from now in a garage, while on holiday in Cornwall," he continued. "You hadn't been driven for many years and were hidden at the back of the garage under a cover."

Then Bill's eyes shone when he described the next part. "When I sit in you, with my grandpa, you suddenly transform into a new car and bring us here, to London in the past. That very thing happened, earlier today, and you drove us here. You are waiting outside the garage, by the pavement now."

Original XK really didn't look any less confused after all this had been explained to him. Bill thought it looked very much like he didn't believe them.

"I think we're going to have to show him, Grandpa," said Bill.

"OK," agreed Grandpa, "but we'll need to be quiet." Original XK's owner had gone into the house and Grandpa was worried he would hear the garage door opening.

Grandpa went over to the door of the garage and softly turned the handle. He pushed the bottom of the door gently and luckily it swung quietly up. Bill realised, just then, that he hadn't known for sure until that point that they could touch and move things in the past. He was extremely glad that they could!

Original XK looked out through the door and gasped when he saw himself outside, parked by the pavement. The two cars looked at each other with their bumper mouths both open in an 'o'. They looked like identical twin cars!

"XK from the future, meet XK from the past," introduced Bill, realising how funny that sounded as he said it and smiling. The two cars remained shocked for a few more seconds but then both smiled and said, "Hello!" to each other.

"Now we'll explain why we're here," said Grandpa, closing the garage door just as quietly as he had opened it.

Chapter Eleven
The Plan

Grandpa and Bill started to explain to Original XK why they had come to find him.

They told him all about the two men they'd seen go into his owner's office and take the photographs and film. They told him that the men had then arranged to give it to somebody the following morning. They explained that they knew where the men were meeting tomorrow and were going to try and stop them. They said that they thought the men were spies. They explained that they thought his owner was the head of the Secret Intelligence Service and that the men were traitors. They told him that they nccded his help.

Original XK listened to all this very carefully and then dipped his bonnet in a nod. "Of course I will help you. What do you need me to do?"

Bill didn't really have a plan and looked to his grandpa to help him come up with one. How were they going to stop them?

Bill was relieved to see that Grandpa looked like he had an idea. He had the look of someone who'd had an idea slowly downloading into their brain, and **PING!**

It was suddenly there and ready to use!

"Original XK, do you know what your owner's plans are for tomorrow? We need to see if we can get him to where and when the men are meeting tomorrow, Knightsbridge tube at 10.30am," said Grandpa.

"I heard him talking to a man yesterday and arranging to meet him at The Dorchester Hotel tomorrow, at 9 o'clock, for a meeting," replied Original XK.

"That's not far from Knightsbridge tube!" exclaimed Grandpa. "How long do you think he will be?"

"I think he told the man that the meeting would be for about an hour," replied XK.

"Perfect, the timings will work! Now we just have to make sure he sees the two men meeting at the tube station. We must make sure that he is suspicious enough to follow them to see what they are doing."

This seemed a little bit trickier.

"But how do we do that, Grandpa?" asked Bill.

"I'm not sure, Bill," he replied.

Grandpa thought hard for another few minutes. Then another idea downloaded.

"When we travel in XK, the other one from the future, he takes us to places *he* wants to show us. *He* drives. I wonder if *you* would be able to take over the driving and take your owner to the tube station at the right time?" asked Grandpa, looking at Original XK.

"I think you will need Bill with you for it to work. He seems to be the key for the magic to make you talk and drive. We will come to The Dorchester Hotel's car park tomorrow morning and get in you when your owner leaves after his meeting. I don't think he'll be able to see us but hopefully you'll be able to take over the driving."

The plan was agreed.

"Now, Bill, I think we should be getting back to my old house to tell the others about our plan," said Grandpa.

"Goodbye, Original XK. We will see you tomorrow," said Bill, waving as they left the garage.

"Yes, see you tomorrow," said Original XK, closing his eyes as the garage door came down.

Bill and Grandpa climbed back into the other XK waiting outside.

"We've got a plan, XK!" called Bill happily as he got in. They explained the plan to XK on the drive back to see young Grandpa and Charlotte.

As they drove down Park Lane and past The Dorchester Hotel, it was already dark.

"That's where we have to go tomorrow," called out Grandpa. They drove past the Park Lane entrance to the hotel with its sweeping forecourt and large sign over the entrance.

As they drove round the huge roundabout that is Hyde Park Corner, Bill could see the Wellington Arch and down Constitution Hill. Looking towards The Mall he could just make out a line of huge steel arches lit up for the night along the famous approach to Buckingham Palace.

He could see a huge grandstand on Apsley House which had specially-built seating from where people had watched the Coronation earlier that day. He could see long, Royal Standard, red flags hanging down from ornate poles with a crown design at the top.

Suddenly, the sky began to light up above their heads, colourful sprays of colour were reflected on the windscreen of the car. Bill tiltled his head back and looked up.

Fireworks! He loved fireworks.

It was the display launched from the Victoria Embankment on The Thames to mark the end of the Coronation celebrations. The fireworks burst in big snowflake shapes all over the sky and Bill gazed at them happily from his seat in XK.

Then they passed Knightsbridge tube entrance on the left. "That's where we need to find the two men in the morning," said Grandpa, pointing out the entrance to Bill. They drove past the huge, round dome of the Royal Albert Hall, past the entrance to Kensington Gardens again and arrived back at Grandpa's old house.

They knew that Grandpa and Charlotte would be in bed at this time, but they also knew that they would want to know what had happened.

"That's my old bedroom window," said Grandpa, pointing at a window at the very top of the house. Bill picked up some soil from the front garden and threw it up to the window. Young Grandpa soon appeared at the window.

"We found XK's first owner's house," Bill called up to young Grandpa from the street below. "He told us where his owner will be tomorrow morning. We are going to try and take him to where the men are meeting the Russian man. Hopefully we can show him what those men are up to. We'll come and see you again tomorrow to tell you how we got on." Young Grandpa smiled and nodded.

"Good luck!" he called down to them, waved and closed his window. Bill and Grandpa got back into XK.

"Back to the holiday cottage, I think now, Bill," said Grandpa. "We need our rest for tomorrow. A lovely relaxing day at the beach will be just the ticket. Besides, I want to see you on this bodyboard of yours." Bill smiled, XK started to drive and they were transported back to the garage in Cornwall and the present day.

"Bill! Dad!" they heard Bill's mum's voice calling from the house. "Are you out in the garage again? Looking at that old car?" Bill looked at Grandpa in surprise.

"I told your mum we'd found the car before I telephoned the owners," explained Grandpa.

"Ah, of course," nodded Bill, understanding now how she knew about XK.

"We're off to the beach now. I've got a lovely picnic lunch for later. Bill you just need to grab your bodyboard and swimming trunks and we're all set."

"Okay, Mum, coming now!" called Bill. Turning back to look inside the garage he said, "Bye, XK, see you tomorrow."

Chapter Twelve
Surveillance

Bill woke up the following morning full of anticipation and excitement for the adventure ahead. He dashed downstairs and found his grandpa already at the table eating breakfast. He looked almost as excited as Bill.

"Come on, Bill. Have a good breakfast. It's going to be a busy day today," he said with a smile and winked at Bill.

Bill grinned back at Grandpa and started on his breakfast. He ate it at some speed again and announced to his mum, "Grandpa and I are just going to the garage again to look at the lovely old car." His mum smiled.

"OK, but don't be too long. Alice wants to go for a paddle in the sea with you. The sun is out and it's such a beautiful day," replied his mum.

"OK, we won't be long," said Bill, already at the door to the garden, with one foot outside. "Come on, Grandpa."

As they crossed the garden to the garage, Bill turned to his grandpa and said, "I hope our plan works, Grandpa."

"Me too, Bill," replied Grandpa. "We've got to do our best to stop those plans getting into the wrong hands."

They reached the garage, opened the doors and went over to XK. Bill pulled off the blanket and XK woke. "Ready, XK?" asked Bill.

"I'm ready," answered the car. He looked just as determined as Bill and Grandpa to make the mission a success.

"Right then, take us to The Dorchester Hotel at about 9.30 am on the morning after Coronation Day. We need to make sure we are there for when your first owner finishes his meeting." XK's engine started and the fog began to swirl around them.

The next thing they knew, they were pulling in to a sweeping driveway in front of the towering façade of the hotel. There was a little circlular garden in front of the hotel with a trickling fountain in the middle.

As they drove around this little 'crescent', Bill saw a big, wrought iron balcony, with a hedge and plants growing on it, forming a canopy over the huge wooden doors. Beautiful, white stone steps led up to these doors and to each side were little potted trees and plants. Standing at the door were smart doormen, dressed in long green jackets and top hats. Bill saw all this as they passed the front of the hotel.

They continued round to the car parking area and Bill immediately spotted Original XK.

"Over there, Grandpa," said Bill pointing.

"I see him, we'll park just in front of him. We'd better not go in a proper space as no-one can see us," said Grandpa.

They pulled up in front of Original XK. Bill and Grandpa got out and went over to him. As they approached, he opened his eyes.

"You're here," said Original XK. "My owner is inside, he should be at his meeting now."

Bill nodded, "I'll go and check."

Grandpa nodded too but said, "Don't be too long. Just check he's there and come straight back."

Bill set off, running back round to the grand front entrance of the hotel. He passed through the big wooden doors, as they were being opened for someone else, and found himself inside a sumptuous, hotel lobby.

Breakfast was set up on the tables in a nearby long lounge, so it didn't take him long to find where he needed to go! The floor was marble, with big carpets placed along it at intervals. Large tables were set up along the middle of the long room, which had plush couches with lots of cushions on one side and comfortable-looking soft chairs on the other.

To either side of these central tables there were smaller tables set up on the sides of the room. These tables just had chairs, no couches, and were placed next to apricot-coloured marble columns that lined the walls of the room. At the top of each column was a golden Corinthian capital and between the columns, huge windows were framed with luxurious velvet curtains. The curtains were the same apricot colour as the columns. Potted palm plants and tall lamps stood on the floor in front of the columns.

Bill walked past the people having their breakfasts at the tables. He was glad he'd had his own breakfast before coming, otherwise his mouth would be watering at the sight of it!

Croissants and juice and toast and fruit and cereal and bacon and eggs and mushrooms and tomato — it all looked delicious.

As he walked down the length of the room, he suddenly saw who he needed to find. XK's first owner was sitting at one of the side tables, facing another man, talking and drinking a cup of coffee.

He was here.

Bill had seen what he needed to and turned to leave the room and get back to Grandpa and the two XKs in the car park. But just as he turned, he knocked his leg against one of the tables in the centre of the room.

The table wobbled, and Bill gasped. A glass of orange juice started to wobble too. Oh no! It looked like it was going to topple over and crash to the floor. Bill held his breath and watched.

The people in the room couldn't see him and would think it extremely stange for a glass of juice to fall over by itself.

Then, his panic was overtaken with a dose of sensible, quick-thinking. He could simply reach out his hand to steady the glass. No one would see him do it.

So he did just that. He reached out, making his hand into a small wall, and stopped the glass just before it tipped — disaster averted!

Relieved, he hurried back to the car park to find the others.

"He's in there," announced Bill as he arrived back at the cars.

"Good, we just need to wait now and hope that the meeting finishes on time," said Grandpa. "We need to get in Original XK now and wait for him. XK, when he starts the engine you need to move to let us out and then follow us wherever we go.

Does that all sound alright?"

The XK from the Cornish garage said, "Yes," and dipped his bonnet in a nod.

It seemed like a long wait, that half an hour, but eventually the man left the hotel and walked towards his car. "Right on time, it's 10 o'clock," whispered Grandpa. Grandpa and Bill squeezed over to the passenger seat of Original XK. Bill was practically sitting on his grandpa's lap, something he hadn't done for many, many years.

They left the hotel's car park and turned out on to Park Lane. XK followed behind.

Driving along, Bill could see Hyde Park on their right. It wasn't a very comfortable ride. Sitting squished right up and half on, half off his grandpa's knee wasn't entirely relaxing.

When they reached Hyde Park Corner, Original XK's driver went to turn left up Piccadilly. "We need to go right here, Original XK," whispered Grandpa. "It's time for you to take over."

Suddenly, Original XK turned the steering wheel himself, pulled to the right and took the turning to Knightsbridge. His driver was astonished.

"What on earth is going on?!" he cried, looking shocked as he lost control of the car. He tried to steer the wheel in the other direction but couldn't.

Original XK was well and truly in control of where they were going.

"And who on earth are you?" he shouted, turning to face Grandpa and Bill, who were still pushed up against the door. Now it was their turn to be shocked.

"Wow, can you see us now?" asked Bill.

"Of course I can see you!" boomed the man. "And I'd like to know just what you think you're doing in my car. And, more to the point, who exactly is driving?"

Once the magic had started driving the car, it seemed that the man could also see Bill and Grandpa! The magic had also made them visible to him.

Just at that moment, they arrived at Knightsbridge tube station. "It's a long story," began Bill. "A bit *too* long to explain now. But please trust us. There are two men who have taken information and a microfilm from a folder in your desk. We saw them take it. They are going to give it

to a Russian man. We know that the two men are meeting here, at the tube station to take it to him. They're meeting at 10.30. That's them, over there!"

Bill pointed to the pavement outside the station. The two men were standing by the entrance to the tube station with their heads bowed, faces mostly covered by their hats, whispering to one another intently. Just then, they lifted their heads a little and everyone in the car was able to see their faces.

"Why, that's Wilson and Clarke! What are they doing here?" said Original XK's owner.

"Those are the men that took the information from your office," explained Grandpa. "It's them we've come to follow."

Just then, Wilson and Clarke started to walk, setting off along Brompton Road. "Quickly, there's no time to explain more, we must follow them," said Grandpa urgently.

"Yes," agreed the man, "I'd like to know just what those two are up to."

They pulled away from the kerb and drove slowly down the street, trying to keep in line with the men so they could see where they went. As they drove, the man couldn't help but ask some questions. "But who are you? And how did you come to be in my office to see what Wilson and Clarke were doing?"

"This is going to sound quite unbelievable," began Grandpa. "But we are from the future. We discovered your car, this XK, in the garage of a holiday cottage whilst in Cornwall. When Bill sits in the car, it magically transports us back in time. No-one else can see us, except myself as a boy and my sister – and now *you*," explained Grandpa.

"We believe that we have been brought here to help stop Wilson and Clarke from doing what they are planning to do. We overheard them talking with the Russian man and what they were planning sounded very suspicious to us," continued Grandpa. "We were able to follow them into your office as they couldn't see us. We realised that they were probably spies, who work for you, and were doing something they shouldn't."

Grandpa explained all this as they travelled along Brompton Road, watching Wilson and Clarke closely as they walked.

"Well, I can neither confirm nor deny that they are spies," smiled the man. "But I *can* tell you, I am very grateful that you have brought this to my attention." Bill was relieved.

"My name is Archibald Winfield-Bell," said the man, extending out his hand to shake Grandpa's and then Bill's. "I think I know what they have taken from my desk and you are quite right; we do not want it falling into the wrong hands."

Just then, Wilson and Clarke quickly turned

off the street and ducked into the entrance of *Harrods* department store.

"Quick, we don't want to lose them," said Archibald. "This is a technique to lose a tail."

Bill and Grandpa exchanged a smile at this, it sounded very much like spy-speak.

"*Harrods* is the perfect place to lose someone following you with all its escalators and different departments," continued Archibald, stopping the car.

"I'll go after them," said Bill, jumping quickly out of the car.

"I'll come with you! They may split up," said Grandpa, following.

They darted past the uniformed doorman and in through the huge, rotating doors. Bill spotted

Wilson and Clarke, as they crossed the entrance foyer and went straight on into the food hall.

Bill and Grandpa followed them through the gleaming food hall, the floors and walls of which were covered with immaculate tiles.

They passed shining, highly-polished glass and metal counters full of all imaginable types of food. Behind each counter there were tall wooden shelves displaying teas and tins of biscuits. On the top of some counters, tins were stacked in large pyramid towers.

Bill couldn't allow himself to be distracted by all the lovely treats on show. He had to keep track of the men. He focussed his eyes on them and followed them through a large tiled and mirrored door into an area full of hats and handbags.

They carried on to the back of the shop and approached an escalator. Bill and Grandpa got ready to step on to it but, at the last moment, one of the men didn't get on. He forked off to the left.

Grandpa said, "I'll stay on him, you carry on up." Bill went up the escalator, following his 'target'.

They went into row after row of women's

clothes. The man forked left, then right, weaving his way through them all. Amazingly, Bill managed to stay right behind him.

It helped, of course, that neither the man, nor anyone else in the shop, could see him.

They made their way back to the front of the store and there the man found another escalator and they travelled up to the homewares area. The man weaved in and out of displays of tables and chairs and beds and linen until eventually approaching the far-side escalators and descending to the ground floor again.

Soon they were back at the hats and handbags, then weaved back through the food hall and to the Brompton Road entrance door again.

There Bill saw Grandpa and his 'target'. They were still on track.

Chapter Thirteen
The Drop

Wilson and Clarke went back out into the street. Bill and Grandpa re-joined Archibald in Original XK and they continued to follow them. The two men clearly didn't know that they were being tailed and were relaxed and chatting to one another as they walked.

Bill was aware that they needed to keep their distance. Original XK was visible to everyone. It was only XK, following behind, that people couldn't see.

Luckily, Archibald seemed to be an expert at this sort of thing and knew just how close they could get without Wilson and Clarke noticing.

They continued, for some way, down Brompton Road like that, following the men at walking pace. As they did so, Archibald spotted a telephone box. "I think it's time I called for some back-up," said Archibald. "You carry on following them. I'm sure I can catch you up."

He leapt out of the car and dashed over to the telephone box. Grandpa took over the driving. It was a quick call and Archibald was soon back in the driving seat. They carried on down Brompton Road, past all the shops. People were going about their daily business and Bill thought how strange it was that they were totally unaware of the exciting adventure he, Grandpa, both XKs and Mr Winfield-Bell were having.

They followed the two men through some railings off the pavement and up to the entrance of a large church with a stone facade. Bill looked up and saw the large, triangular second storey of the building, perched on top of huge pillars,

looming above him with huge statues on top. It looked to Bill like a big, stone wedding cake — just like the one he'd seen at his aunt's wedding last summer.

Wilson and Clarke went up the stone steps and into the porch formed between the front pillars and the doors to the church. Bill, Grandpa and Archibald left the two XKs by the kerb and followed them up. Three other cars arrived and parked in front of the church too. Archibald signalled to the men sitting inside them. It was clear that this was the 'back-up'.

Wilson and Clarke went through the huge wooden doors and stepped into the church. Bill, Grandpa and Archibald followed them in. They were inside a huge, vast church with an ornate ceiling. A spectacular dome was above them and ahead. They followed the two men a short way down the aisle of the church and past rows of pews on either side.

Huge stone archways ran down the length of the church, framed by dark, black marble pillars with gold-leaf tops. Through the archways were small side chapels and Wilson and Clarke suddenly turned off the central aisle and went into one.

Bill, Grandpa and Archibald turned too, and saw them approach one of the statues in the chapel. The man who had taken the photographs and put the microfilm in his pocket now took something out of his pocket and placed it in a little space at the bottom of the statue.

"That's it – that's the drop!" said Archibald.

Suddenly, Bill noticed that other agents from the three cars were right behind them. They suddenly charged forward to arrest the men.

Wilson and Clarke were shocked to see Archibald and quickly tried to think of an excuse for their traitorous actions.

"We were just putting this here for safe-keeping, Sir," one of them said to Archibald. "We received intelligence yesterday that your office was at risk and wanted to move it to a safe place."

It was a pathetic attempt at an excuse, but the men seemed desperate.

"I have witnesses that heard you plotting with a Russian gentleman to steal these plans. Take them into custody please." At this, Archibald turned to the other agents, who placed the men in handcuffs and led them to the cars.

"This is not over; we must wait now and catch the other man coming to collect the plans and photographs," said Archibald, settling himself in one of the pews to wait.

Bill and Grandpa did the same. They waited for what seemed like ages to Bill.

Grandpa told him afterwards that it was about half an hour. To Bill it seemed like much longer.

Then, suddenly, the Russian man entered through the doors at the back of the church. Bill and Grandpa turned but Archibald stayed looking straight ahead, with his head slightly bowed.

"That's him," Bill whispered to Archibald.

"Right, thank you, Bill," replied Archibald. He raised his hand to his forehead, which could have looked like he was beginning to pray to anyone looking at him in the church. It was a signal.

The other agents, sitting in the pew on the opposite side of the aisle, saw — and readied themselves for action. They waited and watched the man go into the side chapel and approach the same statue. He reached down to collect the items from the base of the statue.

The agents swooped.

Suddenly the man was surrounded. He tried to fight. His arms were swinging, wildly, but were soon pinned down to his sides and taken behind his back.

It all happened within a few seconds. Bill marvelled at the speed of it.

The man had been cuffed.

He was led away, back down the aisle and out through the doors to the cars waiting by the kerb.

He was placed in the back of a separate car to the other two men, but not before seeing them and giving them a glare.

Archibald, Bill and Grandpa watched this happening from the front porch of the church.

Turning to Bill, Archibald said, "Thank you, Bill. You have done your country a great service." He had his hand outstretched.

Bill took it and shook it.

"Many thanks to you too," Archibald said to Grandpa. "I think I can reveal to you and you will keep the secret safe, both now and in the future, that these plans are of vital importance to the security of our country." Bill and Grandpa nodded, agreeing to keep the secret.

"They are for a secret bunker under London, to which the Prime Minister can be taken in a time of emergency," continued Archibald. "It will replace those used during the war under the Treasury in Whitehall. Their existence and location are top secret." Bill looked surprised and thrilled to be trusted with this information.

"Stopping the plans from getting into the wrong hands was the right thing to do and the Secret Service thanks you both. The meeting notes in the photographs also reveal the names of everyone working on the project. The names of these agents getting into the wrong hands would put them in extreme danger. I also thank you on their behalf."

Bill was overjoyed. He was so excited to have had such a wonderful and exciting adventure with his Grandpa and XK.

"Thank you, Mr Winfield-Bell, we enjoyed helping you very much."

Grandpa smiled and put his arm around Bill. "Yes, thank you Mr Winfield-Bell. We are glad to have been of service."

Archibald Winfield-Bell smiled at both of them and said, "Now I must take these men for questioning. Goodbye."

At that, he walked away and returned to his car. Bill and Grandpa followed behind him.

As Archibald got into Original XK, Bill said, "Thank you," to the car.

He heard, "You're very welcome," in return.

Bill and Grandpa watched Archibald's XK lead the convoy of cars pulling away from the kerb and taking the men to face justice.

"Now we must get back to my old house and tell the children everything that's happened today," said Grandpa.

As they drove back, Bill was chattering excitedly, "Grandpa, can you believe it? We've just solved a real-life spy mystery!"

Grandpa smiled and said, "Yes, Bill — I believe we did!"

When they arrived back at Grandpa's old house, young Grandpa and Charlotte were playing out in the street. When they saw them, they came running up.

"What happened?" asked Charlotte, eager to hear their news.

"We did it! XK took us to his previous owner's house and we managed to get him to follow the men. He saw what they were doing and they were arrested. So was the Russian man, you followed that day to the phone box, when he came to collect the package," explained Bill.

"Thank you so much for all your help," said Grandpa. "Both of you," he said turning to face young Grandpa. "We couldn't have done it without you."

Charlotte and young Grandpa were thrilled. "You're welcome. It was so exciting to help you and lovely to meet you," replied Charlotte.

"And it was lovely to meet you too," said Bill, smiling at them.

"I think we must go home now, Bill," said Grandpa.

Bill felt sad to leave them, but he knew that he must. They walked to the car, Grandpa started the engine, the fog swirled around them and Bill waved at Charlotte and young Grandpa until he could no longer see their faces.

Bill enjoyed the remaining days of his holiday on the beach, playing with his sister and splashing around in the sea on his bodyboard.

When it was time to leave, he visited XK in the

garage to say goodbye.

"Goodbye, XK and thank you for my wonderful adventure," he said. He hugged XK tightly, stretching his arms across the bonnet as wide as he could reach.

"Grandpa says we'll come back to visit you. His friend is going to restore you and will tell us how you are getting on. When I see you next, I think you're going to look just like you did when we were in the past."

XK looked up at Bill and said, "Thank you, Bill. You have helped me so much and I really enjoyed our adventure together."

Chapter Fourteen
XK Back on the Road

Over the next year, Grandpa's friend kept them updated with how XK's restoration was going. He sent emails with photos to Grandpa and he and Bill would look at them whenever Bill visited.

The following summer they would be returning to the cottage for their holiday. Bill couldn't wait for the summer and the opportunity to see XK again.

A few weeks before they went, Grandpa telephoned with exciting news. XK was finished and would be back in his garage when they went for their holiday.

Bill was so excited.

The weeks until school holidays passed very slowly — even slower than normal.

Finally, it was the day to go.

As soon as they arrived at the cottage, Bill leapt out of the car and ran to the garage. There was a man with XK, who looked splendid— all restored and gleaming with new paint.

"Hello, I'm Charles Bowley, the XK's owner.

Thank you so much for rediscovering the car. We'd forgotten it was in there."

Grandpa had caught up with Bill and was standing at the garage door. "Hello, Charles," he said and the two men shook hands.

"Would you like to take Bill for a drive?" asked Charles.

"Oh, yes, I would like that very much," replied Grandpa. "Thank you, Charles."

As they drove down the narrow lanes of a Cornish fishing village, Bill was amazed. It felt great to be riding in XK in the present day. Lots of people's heads were turning as he and Grandpa drove past in the beautiful car.

When they arrived back at the cottage, Bill was grinning. "Was it fun?" asked Charles.

"Oh, yes," said Bill.

They opened the doors and, just as Bill was climbing out, he heard a voice, XK's, whispering, "Thank you, Bill."

The End

Look out for the next
book in the series...

The
XK
Files:
140

Coming soon....